Mr. Jeremy Fisher

Retold by
Sarah Toast

Cover illustrated by   Book illustrated by
Anita Nelson   Sam Thiewes

Based on the original story by Beatrix Potter with all new illustrations.

Copyright © 1995 Publications International, Ltd.

Louis Weber, C.E.O.
Publications International, Ltd.
7373 North Cicero Avenue
Lincolnwood, Illinois 60646

Manufactured in U.S.A.

8 7 6 5 4 3 2 1

ISBN: 0-7853-2203-5

PUBLICATIONS INTERNATIONAL, LTD.
Rainbow is a trademark of Publications International, Ltd.

Once upon a time there was a frog named Mr. Jeremy Fisher. He lived in a little, damp house among the buttercups at the edge of a pond.

The water was all slippy-sloppy in the pantry and in the back hallway. But Mr. Jeremy liked getting his feet wet, and he never caught a cold in his life.

Mr. Jeremy was very pleased when he looked outside one morning and saw large raindrops splashing in the pond. "I'll dig up some worms and go fishing," he said to himself.

"I will catch some minnows for my dinner. If I catch more than five, I shall invite my friends Mr. Alderman Ptolemy Tortoise and Sir Isaac Newton. Alderman, however, eats only salad."

Mr. Jeremy put on his raincoat and a pair of boots. He took his fishing rod and basket and set off with great hops to the special place where he kept his boat.

The boat was round and green. It was very much like other lily pads, but it was tied to a plant in the pond.

Mr. Jeremy Fisher took a reed pole and pushed the boat out into open water. "I know a good place for minnows," he said.

When he reached the right place, Mr. Jeremy stuck his reed pole into the muddy bottom of the pond and securely fastened his boat to the pole.

Then he sat down and arranged his fishing tackle. His line had a lovely red float. His rod was a stalk of grass. He tied a worm to the end of the line and cast it in the water.

The rain trickled down his back as Mr. Jeremy sat still and fished for a long time. A water beetle came up underneath the lily-pad boat and nipped the toe of one of Mr. Jeremy's boots, so he pulled his feet up out of reach of the water beetle.

Mr. Jeremy continued to fish into the afternoon, but he was getting very hungry. He was thinking about poling back toward the edge of the pond to get his lunch, when, all of a sudden, there was a hard tug on his line.

"A minnow! A minnow! I have him now!" cried Mr. Jeremy Fisher, pulling in his line.

But what a horrible surprise! Instead of a minnow, Mr. Jeremy landed a spiny stickleback fish!

The stickleback flopped about on the boat. It pricked Mr. Jeremy's fingers and snapped its jaws until it was quite out of breath. Then the fish jumped back into the water.

A school of minnows jumped and laughed at Mr. Jeremy Fisher.

Mr. Jeremy sat sadly on the edge of his boat. As he sucked his sore fingers and looked down through the water, a much worse thing happened. It would have been really terrible if he had not been wearing his raincoat.

A great big trout came up from the depths of the pond with a noisy splash. It caught Mr. Jeremy with a snap of its jaws!

Mr. Jeremy Fisher screamed "Ow! Ow! Ow!" as he was taken off his lily pad.

The trout dived down to the bottom of the pond with Mr. Jeremy Fisher in its mouth. But the trout did not like the taste of the raincoat. In less than a minute, it spit Mr. Jeremy out.

The only things it swallowed were Mr. Jeremy's boots. The fishing tackle sank down into the mud at the bottom of the pond.

Mr. Jeremy Fisher shot up to the surface of the pond like a cork. Then he swam with all his might to the closest bank of the pond.

Mr. Jeremy scrambled out of the pond at a place far from his home. He hopped along near the edge of the pond until he reached his damp house.

He had lost his rod and basket, but it did not matter much. "I am sure I will never dare to go fishing again," said Mr. Jeremy Fisher to himself.

The first thing Mr. Jeremy did was to bandage his hurt fingers. Then he cheered himself up by inviting his friends Sir Isaac and Mr. Alderman Ptolemy to dinner after all.

Mr. Jeremy could not offer them minnows for dinner, but he had something else in the pantry to make a good meal.

Sir Isaac Newton arrived wearing a very handsome black and gold vest. Mr. Alderman Ptolemy Tortoise had a lettuce salad in a string bag.

Mr. Jeremy Fisher told his friends about his terrifying adventures with the stickleback and the trout. After that he showed them his bandaged fingers and his tattered raincoat.

Instead of a nice meal of fat minnows, Mr. Jeremy served roasted grasshopper with ladybug sauce. I am told that frogs consider that a special treat, but Mr. Alderman Ptolemy Tortoise ate only his salad.

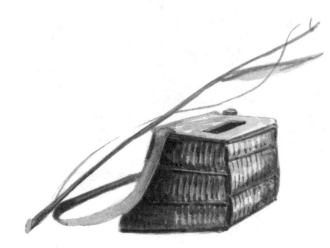